A Christmas Adventure in Little Italy

Written by
JAMES DOTI

Illustrated by
LISA MERTINS

Jabberwocky
Books

Dear Reader,

Imagine a golden angel looking down on you from atop a church. I saw that often when I was a little boy. The outstretched angel wings on the dome of St. Michael the Archangel Church were like a bright beacon, radiating beams of light down on me and all who lived in a neighborhood called Little Italy. It was called that because people who moved from Italy to America made their homes there.

Now imagine it's the day before Christmas. Children are happily riding sleds and throwing snowballs at each other in a park that is shaped like a peanut. That's why everyone calls it "Peanut Park."

Imagine, too, a little boy, watching the snow fall as he looks out from a window inside his grandmother's brown-brick home. His best friend, Blackie, who also happens to be his dog, sits quietly by his side.

You might say, "Blackie can't be his best friend—he's only a dog." But you don't really know about Blackie and that little boy.

This story will help you find out. It's a story that happened more than fifty years ago. And despite the passage of time, the memory shimmers in my mind, just like those angel wings that still glow in the light of day.

Your friend,
Jimmy

Little Jimmy and his dog, Blackie, peer out of a frosted kitchen window, watching the snow lay a white blanket on the sidewalks and streets below.

An elderly woman with a kind smile—Jimmy's grandma—is making cookies. These are special cookies that people from Italy call *biscotti*.

Jimmy turns his head just in time to see her add some chopped almonds to the cookie dough. He calls out, "Nonna! Nonna, can we add some chocolate chips, too?" Nonna is Jimmy's name for his grandma.

"*Si, si, Jimmynuzzo,*" Nonna responds in Italian, using her special name for Jimmy. She shows Jimmy how to hold the large wooden spoon. Then she hands the spoon to him to mix in the chocolate chips. Nonna and Jimmy share a special closeness, so they understand each other without having to speak. And that's good, because although Nonna can understand English, she only speaks Italian.

As the biscotti bake, they give out a sweet aroma of licorice—that's from the anise seed in the dough. It makes the kitchen smell like a candy shop.

Nonna loves to cook and is happy that Jimmy and Blackie are visiting her. Jimmy's mom and dad will join them tomorrow, on Christmas Day.

After the licorice-smelling biscotti have cooled, Nonna carefully places them in cardboard boxes that she ties up with string. Now the cookies are ready to take to the church.

Every year since Nonna first came to America from Italy, she has brought biscotti to St. Michael the Archangel Church. The cookies are then given to poor families on Christmas Eve.

Jimmy gets bundled up in his winter coat and pulls on his yellow rubber boots over his shoes. "It's tough getting these galoshes on," Jimmy moans as he struggles with the large buckles on the front of his boots.

Nonna puts her coat on, too, and wraps a heavy red scarf tightly around her head. Blackie is wearing his red-and-green plaid jacket.

Jimmy tells Nonna, "Look at Blackie's tail. He's excited because he knows we're going for a walk."

Nonna smiles as she looks down to see Blackie's tail whipping back and forth.

Outside, a chill wind hits Jimmy's and Nonna's faces as they carefully pack the containers of biscotti into Jimmy's Radio Flyer wagon.

The little dog shivers from the cold, even though he's wearing his warm jacket. Still, he is excited about going with Jimmy and Nonna on their journey through the neighborhood.

Blackie is most excited about being with Jimmy. They are best friends. They do everything together.

Jimmy pulls the heavy wagon, and Nonna walks at his side. Blackie trails closely behind.

They make their way through the streets of Little Italy, passing under holiday lights. Jimmy can see Christmas trees covered in tinsel behind the snow-draped windows of the homes they pass. Pine wreaths hang on wooden doors.

After they have walked for a few blocks, Jimmy looks back at his dog and says, "Nonna, look at Blackie's tail. It's not wagging anymore. He must be afraid because he doesn't know this part of the neighborhood."

They turn the corner and see St. Michael's Church. It has a tall steeple and a flower-shaped stained-glass window above the doors. The church has a dome topped with a gold-colored statue of St. Michael, the archangel. Spread out wide, the angel's wings appear to glow, even in the gray winter sky.

As Nonna and Jimmy carry the containers of biscotti up the steps of the church, Blackie bounds past them and runs inside, happy to escape the cold wind against his little nose.

The soothing warmth of the sturdy old church comforts them. Candles burn brightly at one side of a stained-glass window.

Sister Mary Teresina gladly accepts the cookies. She tells Nonna, "It wouldn't be Christmas without your wonderful biscotti. Everyone knows you make the best biscotti in all of Little Italy."

Nonna beams with pride. She grasps Sister's hand tightly in hers and thanks Sister by saying, "*Grazie, mille grazie, Suora.*"

Jimmy hides Blackie under his coat so Sister won't see that there is a dog in church. But Blackie peeks his head out, and his nose sniffs the strong, sweet smell of candles burning.

As Nonna, Jimmy, and Blackie start toward home, the sky turns darker and the snow falls harder. Jimmy covers his mouth and nose with his bright blue scarf that Nonna knitted for him, but the icy snow stings his eyes.

Just then, a big green-and-yellow bus comes to a screeching halt by the curb where they are standing. The shrill sound of its brakes and the fountain of slush that sprays up from its huge wheels startle Blackie.

The little dog runs away so fast that he pulls his leash out of Jimmy's hand.

"Blackie! Blackie! Blackie!" Jimmy shouts as he runs after his dog. He sees Blackie dart around a corner up ahead, but by the time Jimmy turns the corner, there is no sign of his dog.

Even Blackie's little paw prints disappear as the snow falls heavily on the sidewalk.

Lost! *Little Blackie is lost!* Tears mingle with the snowflakes on Jimmy's face.

Jimmy and Nonna keep shouting, "Blackie! Blackie! Blackie!"

They trudge all over the neighborhood, desperately looking for any sign of Jimmy's best friend.

As dusk settles, Nonna pulls at Jimmy and, in Italian, pleads with him to return home. *"Andiamo a casa, Jimmynuzzo."*

Just then Jimmy feels a sharp smack on the back of his head. Someone has hit Jimmy with a snowball, spraying icy snow all over him.

Jimmy turns to see a boy laughing and pointing at him.

Jimmy chases the snowball-throwing boy, and as he rounds a corner, he sees his Radio Flyer wagon. He knows where he is now—the wagon is still in front of Peanut Park, where he left it when Blackie ran off.

But instead of containers of biscotti filling the Radio Flyer, the wagon is now piled high with snow.

Tired and cold, Jimmy and Nonna sadly pull the red wagon back home. The thick snow covering the sidewalks slows their journey.

The green and red holiday lights that hang across the streets are now brightly lit, but they bring no holiday cheer for Jimmy.

Jimmy sees a Santa Claus ringing a bell on the street corner, but Jimmy knows it won't be Christmas without Blackie.

Jimmy and Nonna finally reach home, and they slowly climb the steps to the front door.

From the other side of the door, they hear a strange sound.

"What's that scratch, scratch, scratching?" Jimmy asks.

At first, Nonna is puzzled, too. Then a big grin covers her face as she opens the door.

"It's Blackie!" Jimmy shouts.

Blackie's tail whips quickly from side to side as he jumps and slobbers on Jimmy.

"Are you hungry, boy?" Jimmy asks. As he takes Blackie to the kitchen for his dinner, Jimmy sees a note on the table.

Dear Jimmy,
We found Blackie yapping to get inside when we came to bring Nonna her Christmas present. We'll see you later, but hope you enjoy watching your favorite show tonight.
Mom and Dad

Jimmy and Nonna look through the doorway into the living room. Beside the Christmas tree, wrapped in a big red bow, is a brand new television set.

"Nonna! Nonna! Now you have a TV, just like I have at home."

"Mama Mia!" Nonna exclaims with delight.

That evening, Jimmy watches *Captain Video and His Video Rangers* on Nonna's new TV set. As he watches, he dips a biscotti in a tall glass of milk and then takes a big bite of his cookie.

Blackie snuggles close to Jimmy.

"This is my best Christmas ever, now that you're back with me," Jimmy tells Blackie.

Near the warmth of a clanging radiator, Jimmy and Blackie are cozy together. Jimmy takes the last bite of his biscotti, then tips his glass and offers the remaining milk to his best friend, Blackie.

From Jimmy to You

It was fifty years ago when Nonna and I made biscotti together. Now my grandchildren help me make Nonna's biscotti.

You can make these cookies, too—for Christmas or whenever you like! Just ask a grown-up for help.

When the warm, freshly baked biscotti come out of the oven, dip one in a glass of milk and then munch away.

As you dip, biscotti crumbs will fall to the bottom of the glass of milk. I always saved some to give to my best pal, Blackie. He loved lapping it up, getting his nose and whiskers covered in milk and biscotti crumbs—just like my dog, Roxy, does today.

Nonna's Biscotti

½ cup vegetable oil
3 eggs
1 cup sugar
1 tablespoon anise extract, or 3 drops anise oil
3¼ cups all-purpose flour
1 tablespoon baking powder
½ cup chopped almonds (optional)
½ cup chocolate chips (optional)

Preheat the oven to 375°. Grease two cookie sheets.

In a medium bowl, beat together the oil, eggs, sugar, and anise extract (or oil) until well blended. Combine the flour and baking powder in a separate bowl; then stir into the egg mixture. This should form a heavy dough. If adding chocolate chips and/or almonds, stir those in last.

Divide dough into two pieces, and place one on each cookie sheet. Form the dough pieces into rectangles (about 7 x 10 inches) and, using a rolling pin, press down to ½-inch thickness.

Bake for 25 to 30 minutes, until golden brown. Using a pancake turner or large spatula, guide each of the biscotti rectangles onto a wire rack to cool. When the biscotti are cool enough to handle, cut each rectangle into ¾-inch slices, lengthwise.

Lay the slices flat on the cookie sheet. Bake for an additional 3 to 5 minutes, then flip to the other flat side and bake another 3 to 5 minutes, until lightly toasted.

Enjoy the biscotti warm, or cool and store in an airtight container.

Dedicated with love to Nonna Irena Doti and Blackie.

J.D.

Dedicated to the colleagues I shared a rewarding career with
at the Orange County Register.
Without their inspiration, I would not be the happy artist I am today.

L.M.

Copyright © 2010 by James Doti.
Second Printing, 2011

Jabberwocky
Books

Jabberwocky Press
212 3rd Avenue North, Suite 290
Minneapolis, MN 55401
612.455.2293
www.Jabberwocky-Books.com

ISBN - 978-1-935204-08-4
ISBN - 1-935204-08-4

Editorial and Design Assistance by Ann Cameron
Cover Design and Typeset by Kristeen Wegner

Printed in the United States of America

CPSIA facility code: BP 311551